A Very Special Mouse and Mole
published by Graffeg in 2019.
Copyright © Graffeg Limited 2019.

PRINTING HISTORY
Picture Corgi edition published 1996.

Text copyright © Joyce Dunbar, Illustrations
copyright © James Mayhew, design and
production Graffeg Limited. This publication
and content is protected by copyright © 2019.

Joyce Dunbar and James Mayhew are hereby
identified as the authors of this work in
accordance with section 77 of the Copyrights,
Designs and Patents Act 1988.

ISBN 9781912050987

1 2 3 4 5 6 7 8 9

A Very Special
MOUSE & MOLE

Joyce Dunbar and James Mayhew

This book belongs to:

_____

_____

_____

GRAFFEG

For Joy Whitby
a very special human being
J. D and J. M

Contents

Half a Banana

Mole ate half a banana.

He often ate half a banana.

He liked to hide the other half from himself – mostly in a place where he could find it.

Then, 'My goodness,' he would say to himself 'Half a banana behind the clock. What a pleasant surprise! I'd better eat it up.'

And he usually did eat it up, except for the last time, when he couldn't find the second half of the banana. He had hidden it too well from himself.

But that had been yesterday. Today was today. Mole was feeling really peckish and today he was going to get it just right.

He put the leftover half of the banana on the window-sill where it would be easy to find later on.

Then he ate half a biscuit and put the other half in the kitchen drawer.

Next he ate half a crunchy-munchy and put the other half on the mantelpiece.

He ate half a sandwich and half a cream cracker, half a slice of jam roll and half a piece of cheese. He hid the other halves all over the place.

Then he lay down for a nap. 'What a lovely feast will be waiting for me when I wake up,' he murmured.
'A surprise feast for a hungry mole.'

Soon he was snoring loudly.

Then Mouse came in from a walk.

Mouse was feeling peckish. 'What's this?' said Mouse. 'Half a banana on the window-sill. What a pleasant surprise! I will slice it nicely and eat it up.'

Mouse went to get a knife from the kitchen drawer to slice the banana. 'Well, well,' he said. 'Half a biscuit in the kitchen drawer. Just what I fancy.' And he covered the half-biscuit with the sliced half-banana, and ate them both up.

On the mantelpiece Mouse found half a crunchy-munchy, and ate it up. He found half a sandwich and half a cream cracker, half a slice of jam roll and a piece of cheese. Mouse ate them all up. He found all sorts of other things as well. 'Tut, tut,' he muttered. 'How careless of Mole to leave all this food lying around. Never mind, it makes a good feast for a hungry mouse.'

By now, Mouse had eaten so much that he had to sit down for a snooze.

Soon he was snoring loudly, so loudly that he woke up Mole.

'Yum, yum,' went Mole, licking his snout. And he trotted over to the window-sill.

No half a banana.

He looked in the kitchen drawer.
No half a biscuit.

He looked on the mantelpiece.
No half a crunchy-munchy.

He looked in all his hiding places and found no halves of anything at all.

'WHO'S BEEN EATING MY FOOD?' he squealed, so loudly that he woke up Mouse.

'Mole,' said Mouse. 'What have you been up to? I came home from my walk and found bits and pieces of food all over the place.'

'And you saved some for me?' asked Mole.

'Why, no,' said Mouse. 'I ate them all up! I thought it would be a waste to leave them.'

'Mouse,' said Mole. 'That was my half a banana. That was my half a crunchy-munchy, and my half a piece of cheese.'

'Your halves?' said Mouse. 'And I ate them all up! I'm sorry, Mole. But never mind. That means *my* halves must be somewhere. You can have those instead.'

'No, I can't,' said Mole. 'They have been eaten already.'
'Oh dear,' said Mouse. 'I wonder who by? But what's this under my cushion? Another half a banana. It looks a bit ripe, but the riper the sweeter they say.'

'So that's where it got to!' said Mole. '*Yesterday's* half a banana. Would you like a bite?'

'No thank you,' said Mouse. 'You can have it all to yourself.'

So Mole ate it all up.

Preposterous Puddle

On a blustery April morning, Mouse and Mole were out walking. Mouse found a stick to swish. Mole found a puddle to splash in.

'I like this stick,' said Mouse, swishing it through the leaves.

'And I like this puddle,' said Mole, paddling all around its edges.

'I shall give this stick a name,' said Mouse. 'I shall call it Humphrey. There, Humphrey Stick!'

'It looks like a Humphrey already,' said Mole.

'A born Humphrey,' agreed Mouse.

'It has a Humphrey sort of head,' added Mole. 'Now, what shall I call my puddle?'

'You can't give a name to a puddle,' said Mouse. 'That's preposterous.'

'I don't see why not,' said Mole. 'I could even call it Preposterous. There. You have Humphrey Stick. I have Preposterous Puddle. It looks like a Preposterous to me.'

'If you say so,' said Mouse.
'I do say so,' said Mole.

'I have grown quite fond of my stick already,' said Mouse, twirling it round and round.

'And I have grown fond of my puddle,' said Mole.

'I shall take Humphrey Stick home with me and stand him by the door,' said Mouse. 'In time he will become smooth and worn. His head will fit the shape of my paw.'

'Oh, will it?' said Mole.

'I shall take him for lots of walks.'

'Oh, will you?' said Mole.

'We shall become the best of friends,' said Mouse. 'Me and Humphrey Stick.'

'Is that so?' said Mole, pacing around his puddle. 'And what about me and my puddle? I shall take my puddle home. I shall keep him by the door. I shall take him for lots of walks.'

'Don't be silly, Mole,' said Mouse. 'You can't take a puddle home.'

'I know,' gulped Mole. 'It's not fair!'

'Never mind,' said Mouse. 'Enjoy it while you can.

'The sun will come out and dry him up,' said Mole. 'He will vanish into thin air. Can't we do anything to save him?'

'Just you wait here a minute,' said Mouse. 'I have an idea.' Holding on to his stick, Mouse ran all the way home.

Soon he was back, carrying two spoons and an empty jam jar.

'We can put him in this,' said Mouse. 'Then you can take him home.'

Working as fast as they could, Mouse and Mole scooped up Preposterous Puddle until he was mostly in the jar.

'Thank you, Mouse,' said Mole, and the pair set off home.
On their way they met Rat.

'That's a very good stick you've found,' Rat said to Mouse.
'It is,' said Mouse. 'His name is Humphrey.'
'And what have you got in your jam jar?' Rat asked Mole.
'A minnow, perhaps?'

'A puddle,' said Mole. 'And you'll never guess what his name is.'

'A puddle in a jar with a name!' said Rat. 'How preposterous!' And he snickered most unkindly at Mole.

Mole stared at his jam jar. 'This was your idea, Mouse,' he said. 'You have been making a fool of me.'

'No, Mole,' said Mouse. 'I was only trying to help.'

'You did it on purpose,' said Mole, 'but I can be as heartless as you are.' And without another word, he poured Preposterous Puddle to the ground. Then he stomped off home.

The next morning, there was a present for Mole. It was a long knobbly stick. Tied to it was a label. 'Humphrey Stick. Love from Mouse.'

Mole was delighted. 'How kind you are, Mouse,' he said. 'But what about you? Won't you miss Humphrey Stick?'

'No,' said Mouse, producing another from behind his back. 'Meet Ambrose.'

Pebbles

Mole and Mouse were by a pond. They were throwing pebbles into the water.

'I will throw just one more pebble,' said Mouse.

'So will I,' said Mole.

They both threw another pebble, then walked along a little way.

'Why not one more?' said Mouse. 'Why not?' said Mole.

They both threw another pebble.

'Mole,' said Mouse. 'Do you think if we threw pebbles for the rest of the day that there would be any left by the pond?'

'There are an awful lot of pebbles,' said Mole.

'It makes you think,' said Mouse.

'It does,' said Mole.

'What does it make you think, Mole?' asked Mouse.

'You tell me first,' said Mole.

'It makes me think of all the pebbles there are. All the pebbles that have ever been. All the pebbles that will be.'

'Too many pebbles to count,' said Mole.

'And then it makes me think of all the *mice* there are.

And all the mice that have ever been. And all the mice that will be.

'Too many mice to count.' said Mole.

'Exactly,' said Mouse. 'If there are so many pebbles, how can one pebble be important? And if there are so many mice, how can one mouse matter at all?'

'How indeed?' said Mole.

'Mole,' said Mouse. 'That means that *I* do not matter at all.'

'You matter to me,' said Mole.

'But you do not matter either. None of my friends matter. Nothing I think matters. Nothing I feel matters. Nothing I do matters.'

'Stop it, Mouse,' said Mole. 'You are making me sad.'

'I am making myself sad,' said Mouse. A big tear rolled down his cheek and splashed onto the pebbles.

'Now you are making me cry,' said Mole, and two big tears rolled down his cheek.

'Boo hoo,' went Mouse.

'Boo hoo,' went Mole.

'We are making each other cry,' sobbed Mouse. 'You stay here, Mole. I will go and sit over there. We must try to stop crying. Even our tears do not matter.'

So Mole stayed where he was and tried to stop crying. Mouse sat a little way away. Still the tears rolled down. Mouse picked up one of the pebbles. 'One pebble more. One pebble less. What difference does it make?' he sobbed.

Then one of his tears splashed onto the pebble he was holding, bringing out all the colours.

Mouse blinked and wiped his eyes. 'This is a beautiful pebble,' he said. 'It is different from all the others. It is yellow with brown speckles. I will give it to Mole to cheer him up.'

And one of Mole's tears splashed onto a blue pebble, bringing out streaks of white. 'This is an interesting pebble,' said Mole. 'It is different from all the others. I shall give it to Mouse to cheer him up.'

'Mole, I've got something special for you,' said Mouse, giving him the speckled yellow pebble.

'And I've got something special for you,' said Mole, giving Mouse the striped blue pebble.

'Why, thank you, Mole,' said Mouse.

'Thank you, Mouse,' said Mole.

They looked at their pebbles for a moment. Then Mouse said to Mole, 'Are you thinking what I'm thinking?'

'I might be,' said Mole. 'If this is a special pebble, and that is a special pebble, then you are a special mouse, and I am a special mole.'

'What a thinker you are!' said Mouse.

'I am,' said Mole.

And they went home, clutching their pebbles, as happy as happy can be.